Hello Bucky!

Aimee Aryal

Illustrated by Rose Reynolds

www.mascotbooks.com

It was a beautiful fall day at the
University of Wisconsin.

Bucky Badger was on his way to
Camp Randall Stadium to watch
a football game.

He walked down Bascom Hill.

A professor passed by and waved,
"Hello Bucky!"

Bucky went to Memorial Union.

On the Terrace, he ate a scoop
of Babcock Ice Cream.
A couple said, "Hello Bucky!"

Bucky walked over to the Library Mall.

Some students near the fountain said,
"Hello Bucky!"

Bucky stopped by the Kohl Center.

A group of Wisconsin fans standing
nearby waved, "Hello Bucky!"

It was almost time for the football game.
As Bucky walked to the stadium,
he passed by some alumni.

The alumni remembered Bucky from when they went to the University of Wisconsin. They said, "Hello, again, Bucky!"

Finally, Bucky arrived at
Camp Randall Stadium.

He rode the Bucky Wagon onto
the football field. The crowd cheered,
"Let's Go Badgers!"

Bucky watched the game from the sidelines and cheered for the team.

The Badgers scored six points!
The quarterback shouted,
"Touchdown Bucky!"

At half-time the Badger Band
performed on the field.

Bucky and the crowd sang,
"On, Wisconsin."

The Wisconsin Badgers won
the football game!

Bucky gave Coach Alvarez
a high-five. The coach said,
"Great game Bucky!"

After the football game, Bucky was tired.
It had been a long day at the
University of Wisconsin.

He walked home and climbed into bed.

"Goodnight Bucky."

For Anna and Maya,
and all of Bucky's little fans. ~ AA

For my parents, Joe and Elaine, my nephew and niece,
Alder and Annika, my big sis, Julie, and for
Mrs. Remer-Sanez, without whose support these pictures
would not have been possible. ~ JG

Special thanks to:

Barry Alvarez

Cindy Van Matre

For information please contact Mascot Books,
P.O. Box 220157, Chantilly, VA 20153-0157.

ISBN: 1-932888-11-X

Printed in the United States.

www.mascotbooks.com